The story you are about to savor is a
fictional tale with a helping of truth.

*To Emilie and Vivianne,
the greatest little great-nieces
I just want to eat up — A.R.*

*To my grandmother Maria,
for passing down the love of cooking — F.S.*

# Mr. Crum's
## POTATO
## PREDICAMENT

Written by Anne Renaud

Illustrated by Felicita Sala

KIDS CAN PRESS

**George Crum** loved to cook.

He fricasséed and flambéed,
boiled and braised, poached and puréed.
He made sorbets and soufflés, stews and
succotashes, ragouts and goulashes.

George loved cooking so much his house ballooned with food.
So he opened a restaurant called Crum's Place and hired a
waitress with cheeks round as plums, named Gladys.

George cooked to his heart's content, and his customers
devoured his concoctions. Many considered him to be
the best cook in the county.

That is, until one day, when in walked a peculiar-looking patron. He wore a purple polka-dotted cravat and a sunflower on his lapel.

"Filbert P. Horsefeathers is the name," he trumpeted. "The *P* stands for Punctilious. And I have a hankering for a heaping helping of potatoes."

"Just *potatoes?*" said Gladys.

"**Just potatoes,**" said Filbert.

So, with a swish of his apron and a tap to his chef's hat, George got to work. He cut the potatoes into wedges, boiled them, fried them in a dollop of lard and sprinkled them with salt.

Then Gladys set the potatoes down in front
of Filbert Punctilious Horsefeathers.

Filbert speared a wedge with his fork
and peered at it from all sides.

"Too thick," he said, pursing
his lips and pushing his plate away.

"Well, huckleberry biscuits!" said Gladys. "The customer at table five is sending his plate back."

"Picky, picky, picky," muttered George, who had never before had a customer refuse his cooking.

So, with another swish of his apron and a tap to his chef's hat, George prepared a plateful of thinner wedges, and Gladys set them down in front of Filbert Punctilious Horsefeathers.

Filbert speared a wedge with his fork, peered at it, and took a teeny, tiny nibble.

"Still too thick — and bland as burlap," he said, rolling his eyes and pushing his plate away.

"Well, flying flapjacks!" said Gladys. "The customer at table five is sending his plate back AGAIN."

"Fussy, fussy, fussy," muttered George, who proceeded to cook a plateful of even thinner wedges, this time with an extra splash of salt.

When Gladys set the potatoes down in front of Filbert Punctilious Horsefeathers, Filbert speared a wedge with his fork, peered at it, nibbled it and then took a bean-sized bite.

"Still too thick, still bland — and undercooked," he said, puffing out his cheeks and pushing his plate away.

Gladys let out a *tut-tut*, a *tsk-tsk* and a snort, then picked up the plate and returned to George's kitchen a third time.

"This cannot be," said George.
"Everyone loves my spuds.
They are scrumptious. They are
succulent. They are sublime!"

"Not according to finicky, persnickety Filbert Punctilious Horsefeathers," said Gladys.

Now, George was known to his customers to be a bit of a prankster, and his daily menu was evidence of his lively sense of humor. To draw a laugh or two, George often listed menu items that were, shall we say, somewhat unusual.

So, in the spirit of playfulness, George took one more potato and carefully balanced it on his chopping block. With his finest, sharpest knife, he slowly shaved it into the thinnest, slimmest and trimmest of slices.

He heated a ladleful of lard in his pan and fried the slices until they were so crispy they crackled, and then he showered them with salt.

"Let's see how Mr. Horsefeathers fancies these spuds," said George with a wink.

With a wisp of a smile,
Gladys set the plate down in
front of Filbert Punctilious
Horsefeathers.

Filbert turned the plate **this way**.

Then **that way**.

He tried spearing one
of the potato slices, but it
s p l i n t e r e d.

So Filbert put down his fork,
and with his fingers, he stacked the
slices until they **teetered**.

Then he **cracked** one.

And he **snapped** one.

Only after that did
Filbert Punctilious Horsefeathers
pop one into his mouth.

**"PERFECTION!"** he proclaimed.

And before you could say "prickly porcupine pie," Filbert had munched, crunched and gobbled up every last morsel.

"I guess the joke is on you," said Gladys
when she returned the empty plate to George.
"Fire up that frying pan one more time. I want
to try those for myself."

So, with a swish of his apron and a tap to
his chef's hat, George did exactly that.

"Why, my taste buds are tap dancing!"
exclaimed Gladys after sampling George's
new creation.

"Delectable and delicious!" declared George,
after he, too, ate a few. "I'll call them Crum's Crisp
Crispies and put a plateful on every table."

Word spread, and before long, people from all over the county, and far, far beyond, were clamoring for George's new concoction — which came to be known as …

## potato chips!

# Author's Note

This story draws its inspiration from a man named George Crum, who really did exist.

Legend has it that in 1853, while working as a chef at Moon's Lake House in Saratoga Springs, New York, George invented the potato chip quite by accident. Twice, a picky customer returned his fried potatoes, claiming they were too thick and undercooked. As a prank, or perhaps to vent a bit of frustration, George is said to have cut the pieces of potato paper-thin, fried them to a crisp and doused them with salt. He was convinced the customer would turn his nose up at the skinny taters, but to George's surprise, the customer loved them. And before long, people were pouring in for George's specialty, which in later years was referred to as the Saratoga Chip.

Although this story persists and is referenced by a number of sources, George Crum may not have been the first to fry wafer-thin potatoes. Cookbooks published before 1853 feature recipes similar to what George is credited with inventing. But what we *do* know for certain is that George was considered to be a fine cook, especially of fish, wild animals and birds, such as partridge and quail.

*Born circa 1825 in Saratoga County, NY, George Crum was of Native American and African American descent. He died in 1914 and is buried in Malta Ridge, NY.*

*Ad for "Crum's Place" in* the Daily Saratogian, *August 30, 1899.*

He did cook at Moon's Lake House, where crisp potatoes became such a popular dish that customers could order them as "takeout," served in a paper cone. And during the course of his life, George also owned a restaurant, adorned with the sign *Geo. Crum*, which was referred to as "Crum's Place." George's eclectic clientele — which included millionaires, farmers, politicians, heads of industry and laborers — came to him in "swarms, herds, droves and flocks," according to the *New-York Tribune* of December 27, 1891. Today, potato chips are a favorite snack, with billions of bags sold every year. While we may not know whom to thank for cooking the first plateful of potato chips, evidence points to cooks in Saratoga Springs, including George, as having played an important role in developing the snack and making it famous.

*George Crum's restaurant.*
*The man standing in front is*
*believed to be George's son, Richard.*

*Reproduction of a Saratoga Chips box,*
*originally produced by the Saratoga*
*Specialties Company, circa 1902.*

# Acknowledgments

Many hearts and hands went into the making of this book. I wish to thank the following for generously sharing their knowledge and providing guidance: Dave Mitchell, local Saratoga Springs historian and former director of Brookside Museum, Saratoga County Historical Society; Kathleen Coleman, Curator, Brookside Museum, Saratoga County Historical Society; Samantha Bosshart, Executive Director, Saratoga Springs Preservation Foundation; Mary Ann Fitzgerald, City Historian and Archivist, Saratoga Springs; Paul Perreault, local historian, Town of Malta; John Conners, Bolster Collection Curator, Saratoga Springs History Museum; Lauren Roberts, Saratoga County Historian; Teri Blasko, local history librarian, Saratoga Springs Public Library; and Alan Richer, potato chip historian. Finally, a tremendous swell of gratitude to my editor, Yasemin Uçar, whose punctilious advice elevates my work.

# Author's Sources

## Books

Burhans, Dirk. *Crunch! A History of the Great American Potato Chip.* Madison: Terrace Books, 2008

D'Imperio, Chuck. *Great Graves of Upstate New York: Final Resting Places of 70 True American Legends.* Bloomington: iUniverse, Inc., 2008

Kitchiner, William. *The Cook's Oracle,* 4th edition. London: A. Constable & Co. Edinburgh; and Hurst, Robinson, & Co. Cheapside, 1821

Sylvester, Nathaniel Bartlett. *History of Saratoga County, New York: With Biographical Sketches of Some of Its Prominent Men and Pioneers.* Philadelphia: Everts & Ensign, 1878

## Newspapers

*New York Herald*, August 2, 1849

*New York Herald*, July 22, 1852

*New York Herald*, July 27, 1866

*New-York Tribune*, December 27, 1891

*The Daily Saratogian*, August 24, 1897

*The Daily Saratogian*, August 30, 1899

## Websites

http://www.brooksidemuseum.org/2013/10/george-crum-and-the-potato-chip/

http://chipscrumsandspecksofsaratogacountyhistory.com/

http://www.togachipguy.com/

Kids Can Press gratefully acknowledges the financial support of the Government of Ontario, through the Ontario Media Development Corporation; the Ontario Arts Council; the Canada Council for the Arts; and the Government of Canada, through the CBF, for our publishing activity.

Published in Canada and the U.S. by Kids Can Press Ltd.
25 Dockside Drive, Toronto, ON  M5A 0B5

Kids Can Press is a Corus Entertainment Inc. company

www.kidscanpress.com

The artwork in this book was rendered in watercolor and colored pencil.
The text is set in Bodoni.

Edited by Yasemin Uçar
Designed by Karen Powers

Printed and bound in Shenzhen, China in 3/2017 by Imago

CM 17  0 9 8 7 6 5 4 3 2 1

**Library and Archives Canada Cataloguing in Publication**

Renaud, Anne, 1957–, author
    Mr. Crum's potato predicament / written by Anne Renaud ; illustrated by Felicita Sala.

ISBN 978-1-77138-619-7 (hardback)

    1. Crum, George (Chef) — Juvenile fiction. I. Sala, Felicita, illustrator  II. Title.

PS8635.E51M72 2017      jC813'.6      C2016-906426-3

**Photo credits**

Every reasonable effort has been made to trace ownership of, and give accurate credit to, copyrighted material. Information that would enable the publisher to correct any discrepancies in future editions would be appreciated.

p. 34: Photo of George Crum courtesy of Collection of Brookside Museum, Saratoga County Historical Society.

p. 35: Photo of George Crum's restaurant courtesy of Collection of Brookside Museum, Saratoga County Historical Society.

p. 35: Photo of Saratoga Chips box courtesy of Danny and Shelly Jameson, Saratoga Chips, LLC.